Only Silly People Waste

Norah Smaridge

Drawings by Mary Carrithers

Abingdon Press
Nashville and New York

Only Silly People Waste

Library of Congress Cataloging in Publication Data

Smaridge, Norah.
  Only silly people waste.

  SUMMARY: Fourteen humorous poems make a
case for conservation of electricity, toothpaste, paper,
water, bandaids, and other frequently wasted items.

  1. Conservation of natural resources—Juvenile
poetry. [1. Conservation of natural resources—Poetry.
2. Humorous poetry] I. Carrithers, Mary. II. Title.
  PZ8.3.S6370n   811'.5'2   75-15623
            ISBN 0-687-28847-9

For
Lucinda Heidsieck
and
Jennifer Relfe

WELCOME

It's a Waste of Energy

Some boys and girls are smart all day
But not so smart at night—
They waste that precious energy
That's called ELECTRIC LIGHT.

They turn lights ON, so they can see
To play and romp about
But when they're through—and this means YOU—
They never turn them OUT.

Perhaps they kindly leave a light
So ghosts can find their way
Or Batman take a peek inside
Or make a little stay?

PLEASE, when there isn't anything
You really need it for,
TURN OUT THE LIGHT—or pretty soon
There won't be any more!

Then think how scary it will be
On starless, moonless nights!
No friendly lamps, no windows lit,
No winking traffic lights,

Just inky darkness everywhere
(And spooky noises, too)
And people falling over things
And crashing into YOU.

Next Time, Remember

When you've enjoyed your little snack
And put the peanut butter back
CLOSE THE REFRIGERATOR DOOR
(I've said this fifty times before)
Or else the food will go to waste,
The milk will have a funny taste,
The carrots and the salad stuff
Will not be cold or crisp enough,
The jello will refuse to jell,
The pink ice cream will melt as well—
And Daddy WON'T be pleased to meet
Our butter, flowing down the street.

SHOPPING
LIST
eggs
butter

Dentist

ICE
CREAM

Who Needs It?

When you're not watching children's shows,
Funny cartoons, and things like those,
Please save a little energy
By turning off that big TV.

No one has time for sitting down,
Daddy is working hard downtown,
Mom has her club and stuff like that—
The one, lone watcher is the cat.

But Puss is choosy as can be—
She's only waiting there to see
Commercials showing tuna fish
Or Tasty Scraps, her favorite dish.

At puppets, Puss turns up her nose
And, even during Disney shows,
She takes a nap and doesn't stir—
How dumb to waste TV on HER.

Hands Off!

Although you feel a little chilly
To push the heat so high is silly.
You don't NEED ninety-five, now do you?
That's hot enough to barbecue you!

Poor Daddy's face is lobster red,
Mom's hair clings damply to her head,
The pup is panting, feeling queer,
It's like a steamy shower in here!

The fish are wondering how come
It's HOT in their a-quar-i-um,
The radiators bang and hiss—
It's wicked, wasting heat like this!

In future, when you're cold, just go
Pretend that you're an Eskimo
In Mom's big, furry coat and hat
But NEVER touch the ther-mo-stat.

Turn That Faucet Off!

What would we do if EVERYONE
Forgot and let the faucets run
And filled the bath right to the brim
(In case a whale stopped by to swim?).

There'd be BIG trouble by and by
For, when the reservoirs ran dry,
Instead of having quite a lot
We'd have NO water, cold or hot.

No water for the baby's tub,
No way to give the dog a scrub,
No ice in the refrigerator,
No drink to give your alligator,
No way to mop the kitchen floor
Or run the washer anymore.

There'd soon be lots of spots and mess
And children stuck with stickiness—
And even GROWN-UPS going places
With grubby knees and dirty faces!

Toothsome

No need to squeeze out half a tube
Of toothpaste, honeybunch—
Unless you plan to use it in
A sandwich for your lunch?

Put That Back!

A paper cup is meant to hold
A drink of something nice and cold,
It's NOT for making Puss a hat
(She'd NEVER wear a thing like that!).

It really isn't strong enough
For building towers and forts and stuff,
It's not for floating in the bath
Or scooping dirt up from the path,
And can't you find some safer thing
To carry caterpillars in?

Although you know they're not for play
You've wasted lots of cups today.
That's going to make poor Mother sad
And YOU, my friend, will hear from Dad.

What's All That?

Who's in the bathroom?
A monster from space!
Clouds on his head
And a fat, frothy face!

Foam on the ceiling,
The bath mat, the chair,
The monster's exhausted—
He just washed his hair.

He used half a bottle
Of liquid shampoo!
(Who dares to tell him
TWO CAPFULS will do?)

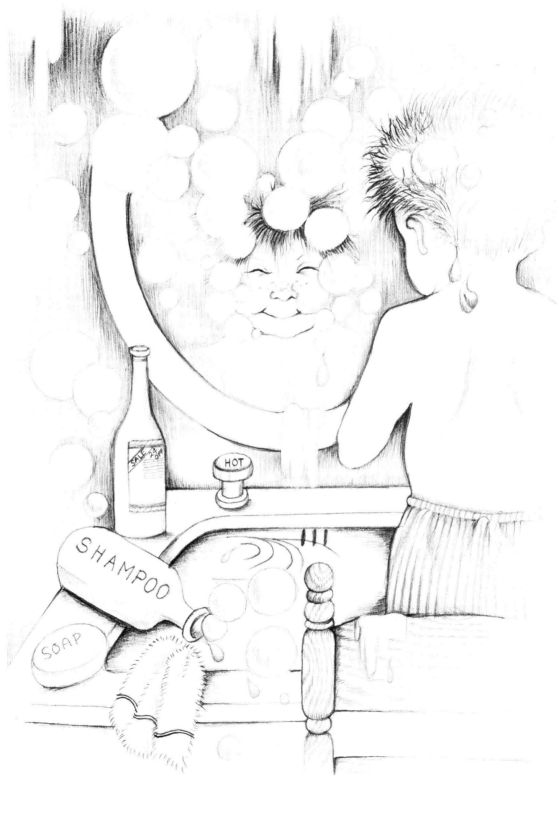

No More After These

The kittens in the nursery rhyme
Each lost his mittens just one time,
But YOU, my dear, have lost so many
It makes no sense to buy you any.

You float them in a pool, I think,
And laugh like crazy when they sink,
Or maybe throw them for the pup
And stand and watch him chew them up.

Or else you park them here or there
Or lend them to a polar bear?
Or—very possibly—you like
To use them polishing your bike?

Well, here's another pair, my pet,
THE LAST YOU'RE EVER GOING TO GET.
They will not tickle, scratch, or itch,
And Grandma knitted every stitch.

They're in your favorite color, too,
So take them—but remember, do,
That if you dare get rid of these
Your paws will simply have to freeze.

Enough's Enough

It costs so much, the time has come
To stop such waste of chewing gum!
You try a stick, and make a face,
And quickly spit it out someplace
Because it's not your favorite cherry
But something queer, called BOYSENBERRY.
You take a piece to chew in bed
But swiftly fall asleep instead,
And when you wake your gum's still there—
But mostly sticking in your hair.

With wads of gum, you fix your truck
Or anything that comes unstuck
And, while that's pretty smart of you,
It would be cheaper using glue.

Starting right now, dear, please get wise
And help us to e-con-o-mize,
SIX sticks of chewing gum are plenty—
Only a crocodile needs TWENTY.

Where Does It Hurt?

If you have tripped, or fallen flat
On jagged rocks or things like that,
Or tumbled from a tree so high
It practically touched the sky,
If a tornado ripped through town
And picked you up and flung you down,
Or if a tiger from the zoo
Escaped and took a poke at YOU—
If THAT'S what hurt you, then it's clear
You really NEED ten band-aids, dear.

But if your wound turns out to be
A scratch that we can scarcely see
And you INSIST on first-aid stuff
ONE band-aid will be quite enough.

Have It Your Own Way

MUST you keep playing with your food?
You surely know it's worse than rude
To spill the milk and leave the meat
That hungry folk would gladly eat?
Let's have no more complaints from you
Especially since they're never true!

The casseroles that Mother makes
DON'T always give you tummy aches;
Your hamburger's NOT full of blood
And gravy ISN'T made with mud!
Gran's cherry pie's NOT full of stones,
Fish NEVER has a million bones,
And those stewed prunes you hate to eat
DON'T look like cockroaches, my sweet.

If you continue, dear, to waste
All food that doesn't suit your taste
Mother is going to go on strike
And YOU can eat the way you like
And live forever as you please
On peanut butter, spread on cheese.

Go Easy

SIX paper towels are rather much
To mop a spot of milk or such!
Don't take great wads of tissues, please,
To cover up one tiny sneeze.
Those paper hankies on the shelf
Are there for you to help yourself,
But don't you think fifteen's a LOT
To wipe the only nose you've got?

Note to an Artist

Woodsmen chop down the forest trees
To make e-nor-mous quantities
Of paper, which is turned with speed
Into a million things we need.
We waste huge piles of paper, too,
And that's a DREADFUL thing to do,
For if we use up all our trees
What's to become of birds and bees?

DO make your drawing paper last!
Try not to color QUITE so fast,
Then couldn't you, before you're done,
Use up BOTH sides, instead of one?
And please don't swipe a double sheet
Of Mom's best stationery, sweet,
For writing HI or LUV TO GRAN
Or drawing her a little man.